Elaine is a primary school teacher in Dublin with a Master of Education degree and is a mum to three young children. 'Treps' was born out of Elaine's experience promoting reading both in the classroom and to her three young kids. Her first-hand experience sees how children positively engage with stories that rhyme, have a sense of magic and have humour. Her love of educating radiates from her writing as it is her intention that children will subliminally learn facts while being engaged in the adventure!

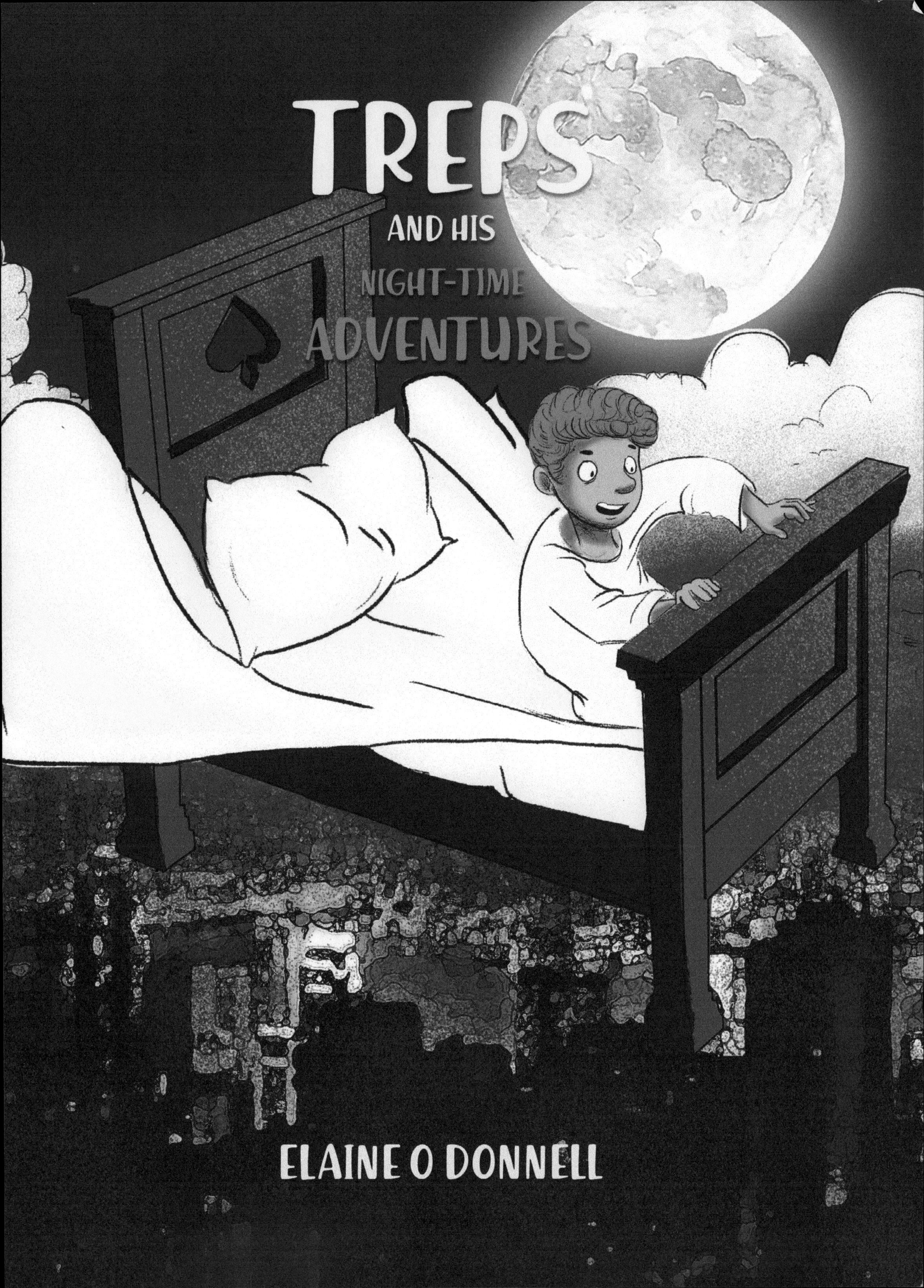
TREPS
AND HIS
NIGHT-TIME
ADVENTURES
ELAINE O DONNELL

A CIP catalogue record for this title is available from the British Library.

ISBN 9781528952590 (Paperback)
ISBN 9781528952620 (ePub e-book)

www.austinmacauley.com

First Published (2021)
Austin Macauley Publishers Ltd
25 Canada Square
Canary Wharf
London
E14 5LQ

To my loves: my husband and kids who bring their own magic everyday
– Paul, Tom, Ruadhrí and Sadie.

Treps was a boy with a secret hidden deep,
where every night when he fell asleep,
he'd enter a world so very unknown
and embark on an adventure all on his own.

Every night in his bed,
Treps closed his eyes and always said,
'Tonight take me somewhere new
so I can learn from a different crew.'

This one night Treps opened his eyes to find
he'd travelled to a place of a different kind.
No longer was he in his bed,
but under his feet were bones, feathers and soil instead.

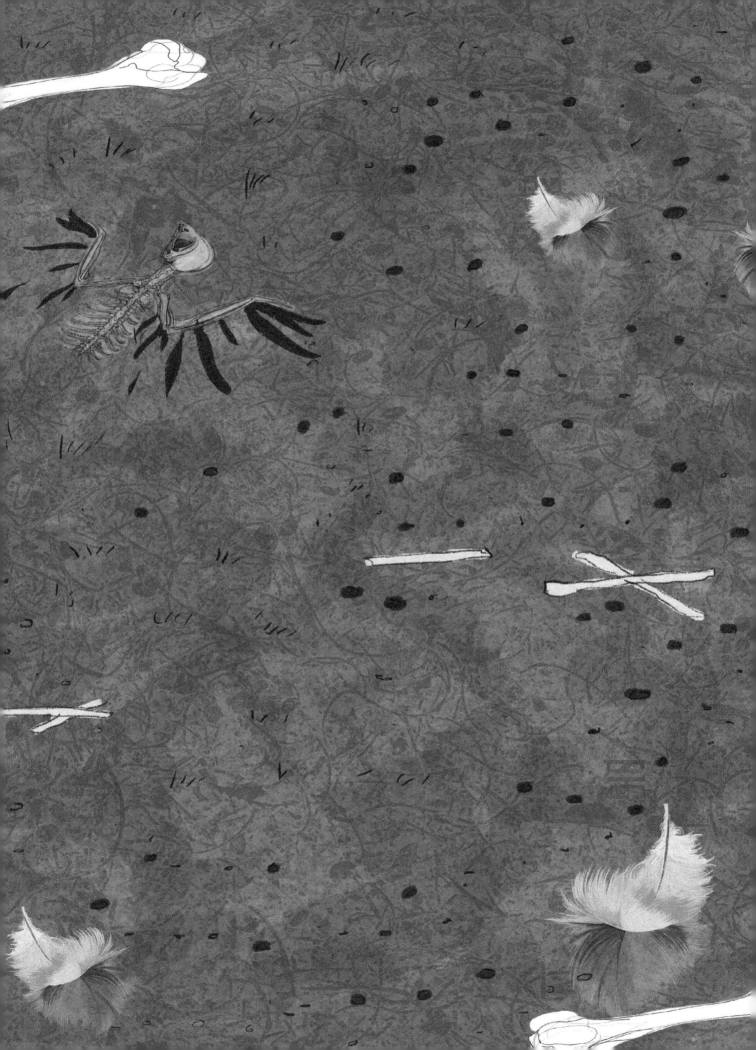

Treps wanted to look around
so took his first steps on this unusual ground.
He then discovered in place of his feet and toes,
he now had four paws, with toes and claws, and fur
that grows and grows.

10

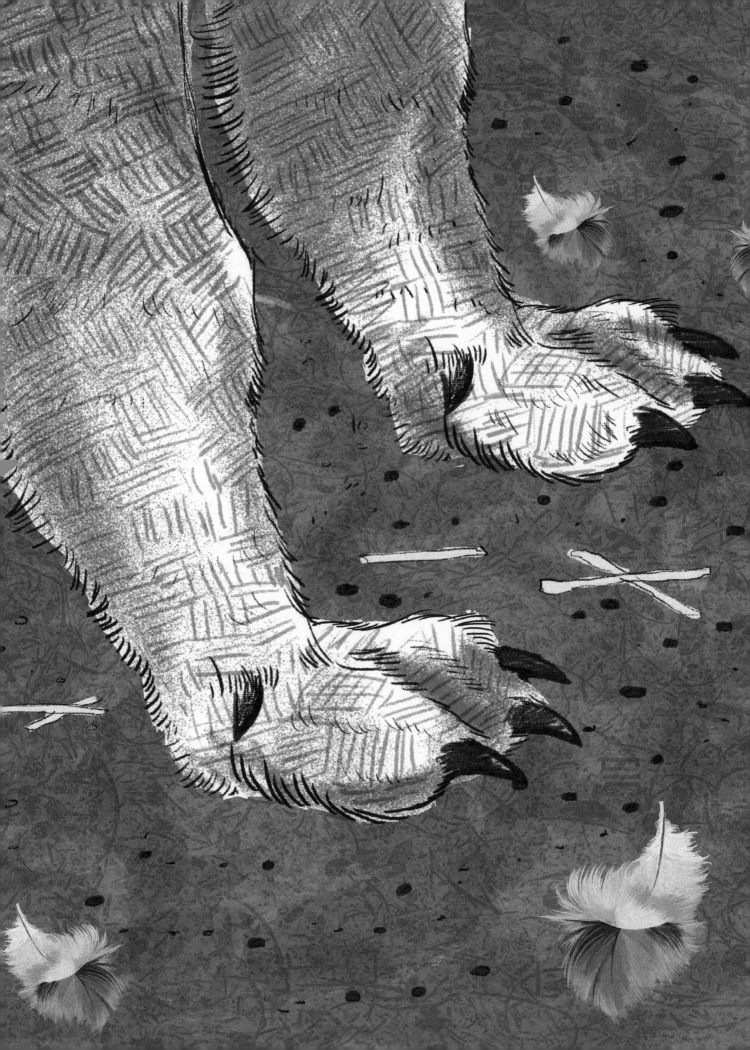

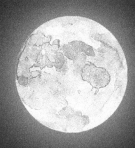

As he took a wander around this hood,
he came upon a lake where next to it he stood.
Looking back at him he saw
two pointy ears, a long snout, whiskers, a narrow jaw.

'What a beautiful orangey-red complexion I sport!
There's really no need to hide in my underground fort.
I'll test these four sprightly legs with socks
and jump and prance while showing off my locks.'

Delighted with his new appearance,
next step was to meet and greet and gain assistance.
He saw his opportunity where ahead was a leash,
so he approached and nervously asked, 'Can any of you teach?
I'm not quite sure where I belong —
am I a dog, a cat or a wolf so strong?'
'Oh, dear little one, what a major fail,
to mistakenly ignore that bushy tail.
You are indeed a curious fox,
whose help we need to food-fill our box.'

'I didn't notice a restaurant, café or deli.
Where do you get the food to fill your belly?'

'Off we must go hunting to catch something nice.
Birds, fish, rabbits or some yummy mice!'
'Surely not now, it's getting dark,'
said a worried Treps who didn't want to take part.
'It's best to hunt at dawn or dusk,
so get ready to stalk and pounce if you must.'

Treps watched the others with their ears to the ground,
listening for any animals making a sound.
Then came the order, 'Get digging! Quick!
I hear our dinner!' The foxes were frantic!

I can't eat this food, thought Treps with worry
and made a decision to quickly scurry,
but stopped in his tracks when met with a wolf who said,
'I'd like to eat you with jam oh so red.'

'Oh, I'm really not tasty,' said Treps to this beast
then began his procedure to be released.

Three wags of his tail, three nods of his head, three flicks of his ears, and he was...

...back safe in his bed.

'Being a fox is not my style.
I'm happy to be Treps ... for a little while!'

CPSIA information can be obtained
at www.ICGtesting.com
Printed in the USA
LVHW071036240521
688313LV00023B/1959